Bloemetje

Bloemetje

a speculative retelling of Hans Christian Andersen's Thumbelina fairy tale

Amanda McNeil

Dedication

To all the women and non-binary people with non-normative families who've supported me in my writing journey. You were at the forefront of my mind when writing this.

Table of Contents

Dedication
5

Table of Contents
6

Author's Note
9

Content Note
12

Glossary
13

Episode 1
16

Episode 2
23

Episode 3
29

Episode 4
37

Episode 5
44

Episode 6
49

Episode 7
55

Episode 8
62

Episode 9
67

Episode 10
73

Episode 11
78

Episode 12
83

Episode 13
88

Episode 14
94

Episode 15
99

Episode 16
106

Episode 17
113

Afterword
120

Author's Note

Fairy tales are originally cautionary tales. Don't go into the forest alone at night. Don't take candy from strangers. Many fairy tale retellings that include queer characters don't update the central caution. It's the same story but with a princess falling in love with a princess or a side character who happens to be queer (ie the gay best friend). While these are valid and important retellings, I wanted to write a queer fairy tale where the central caution is one specifically important for queer families and allies.

Thumbelina was one of the first fairy tales I re-read when looking for one to retell. It was one of my favorites as a child. It immediately struck me how the central conflict in Thumbelina is all about marriage and her rejecting it until the right person comes along (a fairy prince the same size as her, as opposed to a toad or a mole). While at first it seems like Thumbelina is rejecting the dominant culture by turning down marriage proposals, in fact she's reenforcing it by waiting for the most appropriate proposal. I wondered - what would this story look like if the central conflict was Thumbelina consistently rejecting the dominant societal message? Yet I also knew I wanted to tell a story in a queer-inclusive society. I did not want the central conflict to revolve around being queer.

It's entirely possible for a society to be queer-inclusive and yet also have serious issues. When the dominant society is profit-driven, it can be beneficial to "accept" queer people and our families. When you go from feeling oppressed to feeling included, it's all too easy to get swept up into the dominant culture from that rush of being included. This, then, became my cautionary message - don't fall for the belief that your society is beneficial just because it allows you (or others) to be openly queer.

The colonizing society in this book is depicted as coming from a Dutch culture. This was an intentional choice as The Netherlands is one of Earth's colonizing countries. As of the time of this writing, they still have three colonies. I also knew I wanted to feature tulips prominently in the story, and so this colonizer, with its strong ties to tulips, made the most sense of the major four colonizing countries.

The story uses Dutch words for names of jobs, titles, and first names. I've provided a glossary of these words with the pronunciations and translations. You may find it on page 12. It also provides the pronunciation for one flower with a German name and one bird with a Hawaiian name.

Thank you for taking the time to read this note, and I sincerely hope you enjoy the story.

—Amanda McNeil, April 2023

Content Note

If this book was a movie, it would be rated PG for peril, discussion of off-screen deaths, and inexplicit mentions of miscarriage and infertility.

It explores:

- Colonization and decolonization
- Ethical issues in adoption
- Capitalism and corporatocracy and resisting both
- Childlessness (including miscarriage)
- Being childfree by choice
- Different forms families can take
- Personhood for non-human living creatures
- Climate impacts of human activities

Glossary

Aarde - *are' duh* - Earth, the planet

Baseren - *bahz eer' en* - base

Bedrijf - *beh drayf'* - company

Bienenfreund - *bee' nehn froynd* - literally "bee's friend" a purple flower also known as a purple tansy or a fiddleneck (scientific name: Phacelia tanacetifolia)

Bloemetje - *bloom' chuh* - little bloom

Cadeau - *kah dough'* - gift

Grootmoeder - *groot' moo der* - grandmother

Kaua'i 'ō'ō - *kuh wai' ee oh oh* - the name of a bird native to Hawaii that is now extinct

Koningin - *koh' ning gihn* - Queen

Koppeling - *koh' pull ing* - clutch

Koppelingen - *koh' pull ing en* - clutches

Lavasteen - *lah' vah stain* - lava rock

Leidinggevende - *lie ding hayv' en de* - manager [Note the h is a guttural sound made at the back of the throat]

Leidinggevenden - *lie ding hayv' en den* - managers [Note the h is a guttural sound made at the back of the throat]

Nederlands - *nay' der lawnds* - Dutch

Niebie - *nee' bee* - parent, a diminutive form niet-binair, the Dutch word for nonbinary

Oppas - *ope' pahs* - babysitter, child minder, nanny

Peulen - *pool' en* - pod

Raad - *rahd* - council [Note: roll the r]

Rineke - *ree' nuh kuh* - a diminutive form of the Dutch name Rina which is itself a diminutive of the name Caterina. Caterina means pure or beautiful soul. [Note: roll the r]

Van - *fahn* - of

Visie - *fee' see* - vision

Zoeker - *zook' er* - seeker and/or viewfinder

Episode 1

More and more of the woman's colleagues revealed baby bumps. And yet, nearly seven months after the Visie Venus Bedrijf granted reproductive permission to her, she was still bereft. Working six days a week coaxing the terraforming gardens along through backbreaking labor under the dome's protection. It should have felt safe, but all she could sense was the great weight of the Venusian atmosphere pressing against the clear roof like a melting creamsicle. The woman applied to this project so she might have a child. An uninhabited planet was, to her, simply crying out for humanity's propensity to be fruitful and multiply. But she had yet to make it to a bump and its matching announcement. Each of her lost pregnancies remained private. Her beloved, worried for her health, insisted they stop trying for a while. That was when all hope fell out of her body.

She stared at the ceiling of the couple's one-room hut, unable to get out of bed for the second day in a row, running her tongue along the built-up fuzz on her teeth. The doorknob rattled, then hinges creaked as her beloved opened it. A quiet click as they closed it behind them. "Darling," they spoke from the doorway, as if to a frightened cat, "I have a surprise for you."

She did not turn her head to look. The gentle clunk of their boots sounded on the imitation wood floor as they approached the bed. They sat on the edge, and her body tilted toward their weight. A single tear rolled down her cheek, and she closed her eyes, hoping it would make the tears stop.

"Please open your eyes, darling," her beloved pleaded.

Agony's tight grip across the woman's chest insisted upon her bitter, one-word response. "Why?

"I have a surprise for you."

Curiosity bade her open her eyes, finding a dash of bright golden yellow with reddish-purple stripes in front of her. A single unopened tulip.

"What've you done?"

She looked at them just in time to see them shrug. They stood and placed it in a glass of water on their small table. "You couldn't go to the flowers, so I brought one to you."

"You'll be punished."

"A fine at worst."

"But...the dome."

"Will still succeed without it."

Her beloved changed into pajamas and climbed into the bed between her and the wall, both of them on their sides facing the table. They draped one arm over her. Near her belly but not quite touching it. The woman neither cuddled into nor rejected the embrace, gazing at the flower until she fell asleep.

In the morning, after her beloved left for their labor, she got out of bed and approached the flower. As the first light of day fell in through the window onto the bloom, it opened, revealing a tiny baby wearing a gown in the tulip's colors. She looked human, save for her size and points on the tops of her ears. The woman reached into the flower, shifting the baby onto her palm. She nestled in, like two spoonfuls of water.

By the time her beloved returned, the woman had fashioned a tiny cradle from the cardboard box for a box of playing cards and a rattle by filing down the tips of a toothpick and attaching a pistachio shell filled with a few grains of salt. The baby laid inside, cooing. "I've named her Bloemetje," the woman said.

"Little Bloom," her beloved murmured as they gently stroked the baby's cheek with the tip of their forefinger. "You finally get to be Mama"

The woman smiled and came up behind them, encircling their waist with her arms. "And you get to be Niebie."

The next day, the woman now called Mama resumed her labors, bringing Bloemetje along, tucked into her pocket. As each day passed, the couple realized that Bloemetje aged in one day what would take a human child one year, yet her overall size remained smaller than either of their hands.

On day four of being blessed with Bloemetje's presence in their lives, it was impossible for the couple to bring Bloemetje with them to their labors. She was incapable of staying quiet, asking questions every few moments. Although Niebie tried to take a turn staying with Bloemetje, Mama refused to be separated from her and so remained home from her labors yet again.

Bloemetje sat on the table, playing with a tiny stuffed bee Mama had sewn for her. Her tulip sat in a glass nearby, and she looked at it sometimes, its presence reassuring her in a way unlike Mama's or Niebie's. But then, one of the petals fell. Bloemetje pulled herself up and went to it. She grasped the petal with one hand, lifting it up, "Why?" she asked with tears pooling in her eyes.

Mama's mouth dropped open. How did her tiny little girl pick up a petal almost as large as her? But she focused on her child's emotional issue at hand. "No bloom can last forever. They're fleeting. So we should enjoy them while we can." She reached out a fingertip and brushed a tear from Bloemetje's cheek. "There will be other flowers. There are other flowers." But she continued to cry. Mama scooped her into her palm and rocked her gently back and forth.

A knock sounded on the door. Mama paused in her rocking. Bloemetje hiccuped. The knock came again. "Leidinggevende inspection," called a deep voice. And then the day, having already transitioned from good to difficult, became downright terrible.

Mama brought Bloemetje up to her eye level. "Darling, you must become and remain quiet. It's very important. Something bad could happen to you...or to me."

Bloemetje hiccuped one more time as she stopped crying, her eyes growing wide. She nodded. Mama called out to the door, "Just a moment. I'm...not well. Just a moment." She opened a cupboard door and placed Bloemetje in a bowl on a shelf inside. "If anything happens to me...wait here for Niebie." Bloemetje nodded, and Mama closed the cupboard door. But

Bloemetje could still hear.

Episode 2

From her place hidden inside the cupboard, Bloemetje heard Mama's footsteps approaching the hut's door. Then the knob rattled and the door creaked as it opened. One set of clunking steps sounded like Niebie's boots. A second set of steps went clack-clack. Bloemetje wanted so much to see the shoes that made such a sound, but she stayed where she was.

The deep voice spoke again, "You look alright to me."

Two steps sounded then Mama's voice came from somewhere lower, next to the table. "I'm quite weak. As you can see, I can't stand very long."

Another voice spoke, this one high and percussive, "Have you been eating?"

"Yes, of course, I know my duty to Bedrijf."

"You were thoroughly checked by the doctor after your last miscarriage, correct?" The deeper voice resumed.

"Yes," Mama's voice came out a mere whisper.

"Then this cannot be a physical malady," the higher voice continued. "If you are…unable," this dripped with malice, "to return to your labors tomorrow, we'll have to bring you to stay with the ship's psychiatrist."

A silence stretched out so long that Bloemetje worried they'd already taken Mama away.

"Do you understand?" the higher voice asked.

"Yes, Leidinggevende, I do."

The two sets of footsteps began to walk away but then stopped. The deeper voice spoke. "Oh, also, you owe Bedrijf time for the days you've missed. No days off until you've made those up. Understood?"

Mama's voice responded, flat as the tabletop Bloemetje played on that day. "That's only fair."

"Good," the deeper voice responded. "Enjoy the rest of your day." The footsteps retreated, and the door snicked closed. Bloemetje waited what felt like a very long time before the cupboard door opened, and Mama drew her out. Mama's face was wet, so she knew she'd been crying, but she wasn't at the moment. "Well. Let's enjoy the rest of our day, shall we?" And Bloemetje pretended to, because Mama wanted it so badly, but her heart hurt the whole time.

The following day, Mama prepared to return to her labors with Niebie. She leaned down to Bloemetje, now about the length of half her hand. "You must be quiet, my darling, or we could get in trouble." Bloemetje nodded somberly, her pigtails bouncing. Then Mama placed her into her pocket.

So Bloemetje spent each day in Mama's pocket, catching glimpses of the world outside from time to time when Mama moved and the pocket gaped open. The green of the plants. The orange-yellow of the sky above the dome. The light blue fabric on the side of Mama's arm.

Mama and Niebie spoke to each other, ostensibly making commentary, but really teaching Bloemetje. Together, they narrated all their activities. Turning the soil, propping up floppy plants with stakes, watering manually with little jugs where needed. And they told Bloemetje about the planet they came from - Aarde. The plants and animals that once inhabited it before extinction started to occur. Bloemetje loved these stories. Of the plants especially.

On day six, when they got home, and Mama placed her on the table while Niebie reached into a cupboard, pulling out her bed and chair, she said, "I want to see."

"See what?" Mama asked, absentmindedly while she mixed sugar water for Bloemetje. It seemed to be all that the little one needed.

"The plants."

"You know you can't come out of my pocket, dear."

Tears began to well in her eyes.

Niebie set Bloemetje's furniture next to her. "Hey now, we can do something safer and just as good." She sniffled, fighting back the tears. Niebie pulled out one of the big chairs next to the table and sat. "Mama, hand me my tablet, please." Mama did so, and Niebie introduced

Bloemetje to the wondrous world of books full of pictures and even some videos of Aarde's plants and animals. Including the ones that had gone extinct. Sometimes the books and videos called it Earth, but Niebie said it was a different word for the same place. Bloemetje especially loved looking at the tulips but she was also particularly fascinated by bird books.

"Are there any here?" she asked.

"No." Niebie answered, their face falling like the petals dropping off Bloemetje's tulip.

Mama pulled out a chair and sat too. "Bedrijf thought they would eat too many of our crops. And they were right." She looked sternly at Niebie.

But later that night after Mama was asleep and Bloemetje was on the cusp of dreams, Niebie appeared next to her. They leaned down and whispered, "I had a pet budgie - a bird - on Aarde. I inherited it from my mama. Your Grootmoeder. When we left to come here, Bedrijf made me leave it behind. I've never understood. A pet bird wouldn't bother the crops." Niebie's voice broke. Then they kissed the tip of their finger, touched it to Bloemetje's forehead, and went back to bed. Bloemetje's stomach twisted. Why did Bedrijf always seem to make Mama and Niebie sad?

Episode 3

A full week passed with no interference from or mention of Bedrijf. Bloemetje was now thirteen days old and, much as she loved Mama, she wanted to spend some time away from her too. She asked the evening of day thirteen, "Mama, tomorrow may I get out of your pocket?"

"No, darling, it's not safe."

"But I'm bored. I want to see new things."

Niebie offered their pocket, and both Bloemetje and Mama begrudgingly agreed, but day fourteen showed Bloemetje that a day in Niebie's pocket was quite similar to one in Mama's. The same conversations overheard. Identical glimpses of greenery and yellow-orange sky. Frustration fomented in her belly throughout the day and when Niebie placed her on the tabletop in the family's hut then asked, "Was that better?" she wasn't able to hold it in any longer. The no erupted out of her like a murmuration of birds taking off all at once. Mama placed a palm on her head and opened her mouth but before she could speak, Niebie turned to her, "Why don't you go for a walk? I've got this."

Mama lowered her hand, leaving a small smear of dirt on her forehead. "That's fine by me. Pieter has been asking me to stop by for days now. It'll look better if I do."

"Plus you're good friends," Niebie added.

Mama gave a small smile. "Yes, that too." She picked up her bag, told them both she'd be back for dinner, then walked out the door.

Niebie turned back to Bloemetje who'd been standing in the same position she'd landed in after her explosion - arms crossed in front of her with teeth clenched. A small part of her didn't want to remain mad at Niebie. It was difficult to ever remain mad at them. Something about their nature was naturally soothing. But she clung on to her anger with all of her adolescent willpower.

"Bloemetje," Niebie said, pulling up their chair and sitting down so they were at eye-level with her, "would you like to tell me how you're feeling?"

And with that simple invitation the anger flowed out of her, revealing the hurt beneath. "I'm bored, Niebie."

They nodded.

"And I'm..." She reached up a hand and touched the tip of one ear. "I'm different from you and Mama."

Niebie nodded again. "That's true. And I'm different from you and Mama too. And Mama's different from us as well."

Bloemetje pursed her lips. "There's a lot more about me that's different from the two of you."

"Well, you're certainly younger than us both," Niebie considered, tapping a finger against their chin.

"Not that." Bloemetje tried to sound exasperated but a part of her was continuing to soften. "I'm so much smaller than you."

"You are a child still."

She sighed. "It's obvious I'm not going to grow to be as

large as you."

Niebie nodded. "That's true. But I'm also never going to grow as tall as Mama. Do you think that makes me worth less than her?"

"No, but you're much closer to her size than I am to yours."

"I'm sure God made you the size you are for a good reason. Beyond the fact that your size has helped us keep your...unexpected arrival a secret from the Bedrijf."

Bloemetje thought about this, and Niebie let her for a time. Then they continued, "Consider the birds you see on my tablet. They're all many different sizes. And the sizes they are are just the right sizes for them to be. From the smallest sparrow to the largest ostrich. Now, we don't know your purpose yet. But God will show it to us eventually. We just need to keep our hearts and minds open."

"Ok, I guess you're probably right about that," Bloemetje conceded. "But what about my ears? And what about how I'm the only one like me? There's no bird who's the only one like that bird."

"To feel you are the only one is a sad feeling, indeed. I felt that way too, once, when I first approached your Grootmoeder to tell her that I didn't feel like the gender I was assigned at birth."

"She hadn't already explained that you might feel that way? Like you and Mama explained to me?"

"No, she hadn't. Her generation didn't always do it that way."

"Oh." Bloemetje dropped her head slightly. "I see."

"Something else you might not have thought about yet because you only interact with Mama and me is that, while some other families do have a nonbinary parent like myself, most don't. In fact, only about three out of every one hundred people are nonbinary. So, even though, compared to you, I knew a lot of people, I didn't actually know anybody else who was nonbinary too. So I felt alone and scared when I told your Grootmoeder. But after I told her, this is what she said. 'You sound so sad about who you are. You've reminded me of the Kaua'i 'ō'ō bird. A very small black and brown bird with a slightly curved beak that lived on an island. Many years ago, scientists realized that there was only one left. He was a male, and they recorded him singing the call his species made to find a mate. And it was tragic because no one was ever going to respond. Because he was the last of his kind. You sound as hauntingly sad as that Kaua'i 'ō'ō bird's unanswered mating call. But, unlike that bird, you are not alone. You feel different from everybody else but you're not a Kaua'i 'ō'ō bird in a forest full of cardinals. You're a duck among other ducks all of whom are a little different from each other. But they're still ducks. And some ducks care if one duck has curly tail feathers or a quack that sounds more like a peep. But other ducks don't. And I'm a duck who not only doesn't care that you're one of the rarer ducks, I'm a duck that's honored to have been entrusted by God to take care of such a duck.'" Niebie paused and looked up at the ceiling then back at Bloemetje. "The metaphor kind of fell apart at the end," they laughed, and Bloemetje joined them. "But the point remains. Don't let your brain tell you that you're all alone and will remain that way. You have me. You have Mama. You have all of Venus. In fact, you have our whole universe to explore, if you want. Many years ago gender nonconforming people felt very alone. Now we know we're not. Society has embraced us and many people love us just the way we are. I suspect that eventually we'll find others like you. But even if we don't, you're not alone just because you're different. Mama and I will always be here for you."

Tears pooled in the corners of Bloemetje's eyes. Niebie held out their hand, and Bloemetje took a few running steps to it and embraced two of their fingers. Niebie stroked the back of her head with the finger of their other hand. "Thank you, Niebie,"

"I love you, Bloemetje."

"I love you too."

"And hey, listen," Bloemetje looked up at them, her face streaked with tears. "I didn't forget what else you said. About being bored. You are growing up fast, and it's natural to want to see and do more. It's a complicated situation. But I do agree that we can't keep you hidden from the Bedrijf forever."

"Really?" Bloemetje released their fingers and jumped up and down.

"But," Niebie held up a finger, "we'll need to be cautious and thoughtful about how we approach it. I'll start talking about it with Mama, and, in the meantime, ask each day for a bit more freedom to roam. We'll convince her, then we'll figure out a way to do it safely."

Bloemetje agreed, then asked to see the Kaua'i 'ō'ō bird and hear the recording of his mating call. So Niebie got their tablet, and they snuggled up together on the bed to look and listen, and that's how Mama found them when she arrived back home.

Episode 4

The next morning, which was Bloemetje's fifteenth day, she woke to find she was now the same height as Niebie's hand. She stretched then made her request again as Mama reached for her to place her in her pocket. "Please, I don't want to stay in your pocket all day. I want to see." But it wasn't just seeing. She wanted to touch the plants. To sit close to them and breathe them in. She craved it with her whole body like her mouth craved a drink of water upon waking.

"It's not safe," responded Mama, slipping Bloemetje into her pocket once again.

"She's almost grown," pointed out Niebie, "we'll have to tell someone soon."

"God only knows what they might do to her," Mama whispered back. But Bloemetje heard. She always heard her parents' whisperings.

When they arrived at the garden, Bloemetje clenched her jaw. It wasn't fair. She wasn't a child anymore. And even though Niebie understood, they still thought it was too dangerous to just start letting Bloemetje go about the dome. If she could just slip out and for a day, both of her parents would see it was safe. And even apologize to her for being so worried. Then she could explore all the time. But first she needed to find a way out.

She sat wishing for it. After a while, she spotted a loose thread. Grabbing it, she climbed. Her head poked over the pocket's edge, and she saw the whole dome extending around her. Greenery, dirt, dots of color from the flowers, and the full expanse of the dome overhead frosted with the yellow-orange Venusian atmosphere.

Just then, Mama bent over, and Bloemetje fell, almost gracefully, out of her pocket into the dirt.

Bloemetje stood, brushed herself off, and darted off the path behind a tomato plant, its grassy, yet slightly spicy, scent tickling her nose. She knew the vegetable plants lived partway between the dome's outer edge and middle. Where she wanted to be was with the tulips on the outer edge. She walked toward them, furtively at first but less cautiously as time went on.

Before she knew it, she was at the base of a living tulip. A few more steps forward, and she was surrounded by them. Her heart raced in her chest, and she ran along the line of multicolored blooms, her hair, two braids since her thirteenth day, flying out behind her. She skidded to a halt and wrapped her arms around one's base. It didn't quite look like the bloom she came from, but at least it was a pretty yellow.

Just then, a real live bumblebee approached. "Who are you?" she demanded.

"Bloemetje."

"You're not on my roster." She held out a foreleg, reading an imaginary piece of paper.

Bloemetje giggled. "This is my first day out and about."

"I must tell the Koningin." She buzzed away. Bloemetje shrugged and sat at the tulip's base, gazing out at the rest of the garden. Inside the tulip border were more flowers specifically for bees–bleeding hearts, poppies, bienenfreund, and more. The vegetables came next, followed by berry shrubs. At the center were young saplings. Niebie told Bloemetje when she was ten days old that the Bedrijf's highest ranking scientists selected these trees carefully for their speed of growth paired with short stature. "Not unlike you, my little sapling," they commented, tickling her.

The fall of small footsteps drew her out of the memory, and from the flowers came many people of all colors about her size and with ears that rose to pointed tips just like her own. Her heart raced as she realized that, just like Niebie had said, it was not solely her parents' love that made her unlike the Kaua'i 'ō'ō bird but also the existence of others of her size and features.

A woman, slightly taller than Bloemetje, with gray hair in a braided crown and jewels accentuating the tips of her ears, held a scepter and stood at the center of the tiny crowd. Bloemetje scrambled to her feet. Before she could speak, the woman stepped forward and cupped her face with a hand. "Our daughter has returned."

Bloemetje bristled. "I'm not your daughter." No amount of joy at no longer being the only one like herself could make her forget Mama and Niebie's love.

The Koningin shrugged. "That's technically true. Your parents donated you to the Venus bulbs, to be raised by myself and our Oppas." She gazed fondly at an older man about Bloemetje's height with graying temples standing nearby.

"What?"

"Dear," she moved her hand to clasp Bloemetje's, "we are all flower fairies. Without us, tulips cannot bloom."

Bloemetje wanted to protest that this must all be a giant lie, but something in her soul told her it was right.

"We're born out of the tulip's blooms," the Koningin continued. "Our first spring is our childhood. When the blooms fade from the tulips, we're grown and our aging slows. We seek out our own beloved or beloved. It takes at least two standing together over a bulb to cast the spell that creates a baby. Their birth is what makes the tulip bloom the next year. When those babies reach maturity, those of us from the previous year start to pass away. Only a very few make it to three springs. Those of us who do are highly revered elders."

Bloemetje thought about Mama murmuring to her in the evenings how all she'd wanted was a child, and God had sent her. Now the Koningin was telling her in just a short time she'd be finding a beloved and making a child of her own. But although Bloemetje loved the tulips and very much wanted one to care for once again, she knew that she didn't want to make another flower fairy like herself. The desire to be someone's mama was simply absent from her heart. "Does everyone make babies?"

The Koningin blinked. "Yes."

Bloemetje thought for a moment. "What if there's an odd number of fairies?"

"Not everyone desires to be in a couple. Some prefer a throuple or more. Any grouping of beloveds can together make a baby. While a couple is the most common, throuples, quads, and more do exist. God always seems to make the exact logistics work out."

"What about...is there ever a fairy who doesn't want to make a baby?"

The Koningin lifted a quizzical eyebrow. "Of course not. That wouldn't be natural."

Bloemetje's eyes briefly narrowed, then she shook her head in confusion. "Well, it must be. Because I don't want to."

The crowd of flower fairies gasped. The bumblebee buzzed and bobbed up and down. The Koningin raised her hand. "Our daughter was stolen from us. Not raised among us. This is a trauma response. We'll help her heal. Come," she gestured to Bloemetje, "for today, let's focus on celebrating your return."

But Bloemetje, not in the mood to go from one set of grown-ups telling her what to do to another, protested, "No, I won't come with you."

"What will you do then? Return to living in a human's pocket?"

Episode 5

Tears filled Bloemetje's eyes at the Koningin's words, and she turned and ran away, deep into the garden until she couldn't anymore, collapsing at a pepper plant's base, sobbing. A few minutes later she looked up at the sound of a soft footfall sounded, and wiped her eyes. The Oppas held a handkerchief out. "I won't come with you," she said.

"I'd never make you do anything you didn't want to do." His voice was gentle and kind, so she took the handkerchief. "May I sit with you?"

She nodded.

He sat beside her. Near but not too close. "The Koningin is a good person. So are your parents. Neither are to blame for what's occurred."

"You mean for me being unnatural?" She said this with mocking disdain.

"For you not knowing your heritage. The Koningin acts like this," he gestured at Venus, "is natural for us, but it's not. When the Bedrijf gathered bulbs for their project, we knew we couldn't take the risk of hiding an entire generation of flower fairies with them. The Koningin and I volunteered to go as we're both widowed and approaching our third spring. The younger generation could stay and make a separate generation for Aarde. But sending children without their parents was a terrible compromise. Even if your Niebie hadn't plucked your bloom, you wouldn't have had a natural flower fairy childhood."

Bloemetje shifted, sniffling.

"This Bedrijf - like the companies that run Aarde - creates an unnatural setting for humans. Your human parents should've had a society to help them with their loss and childlessness. But instead of societies, humans have allowed these companies to take over. All they care about is profit. And that creates a cruel, lonely, and harsh culture."

"The Koningin seems harsh," Bloemetje muttered.

"The Koningin feels great guilt over what happened to you, and she thinks she must recreate our culture here exactly the way she remembers it. But I remember things she doesn't." He waved his hands in the air. Sparkles came from them, and a tiny yellow buttercup appeared. He tucked it behind one of her ears. "In my youth, I was part of a throuple. One of my beloveds came to us from another field. An uncommon thing. But it does occur. He told me a story his field had. Of a flower fairy who didn't want to help make the blooms. It felt to him that it went against his nature. So the field accepted this and let him decide what he would do with his life."

"What did he end up doing?"

"Well, this field suddenly found themselves missing bees. Something happened to the hive nearby. Without them, everything was simply wrong. So he volunteered to look for more to bring to the field. He adventured far and wide and finally found some bees who were willing to move. He guided them to his own field and brought great healing."

"But you have bees. And I do want to make flowers. Just not babies."

He sighed. "My point isn't quite that literal, my dear. My point," he reached out a hand and lifted her chin up slightly, gazing lovingly into her eyes, "is that God knows exactly what each generation needs. I don't know what your role will be, but I do know that this adventure on Venus demands difference. Even the Koningin and I are doing a different thing right now. It takes a fairy with a lot of organization and a calling to many children to raise an entire generation of them without the help of their parents. At the end of the day, you have to know where you came from and who you are in order to decide who you will be."

Bloemetje stared off beyond the tops of the vegetables and flowers to the dome's arch and Venus's atmosphere beyond, spotting an area that was similar to the color of the stone-ground mustard Niebie put on their sandwiches. Her throat tightened. She escaped one pocket to another slightly larger one.

The Oppas stood. "Come to the party. It'll be a lot of fun." He extended a hand to her.

Just as she took it and stood, she spotted Mama down the row of pepper plants, bending down repeatedly, her lips forming the shape of Bloemetje's name. "I must speak with my parents first. At their lunch break so they don't get in trouble. Will you come with me? It'll be easier to explain with another fairy." She bit her lower lip. But she needn't have worried, for he agreed right away.

Together, they walked to the dome's edges where the Bedrijf's employees lunched. They didn't provide an area in the middle of the garden like one might expect, for leidinggevenden were concerned they might damage a plant in their thirty minutes of relaxation.

Soon, Bloemetje spotted Niebie and Mama sitting on their own, as usual. Their food sat in front of them, untouched, as their eyes skimmed furtively back and forth across the dome, looking for Bloemetje..

Episode 6

Bloemetje walked to the edge of the tulips and called to her parents. Mama darted two steps forward, hand outstretched, with the same energy as a mama duck pursuing a duckling that's fallen behind. But Bloemtje stepped back, hiding behind the tulip's stem. "No, Mama, we need to talk."

"Don't tell me what we need to do; I'm the parent." Mama put her hands on her hips. Niebie came up behind her, whispered in her ear, and Mama lowered her hands. "I'm sorry. We were worried. But you're your own person, and you deserve to be heard. Tell us what's going on."

So Bloemetje told them everything, with the Oppas stepping forward as proof of the other fairies. Mama turned to Niebie, crossing her arms. "How could you steal someone else's child? I never wanted that…" Her voice broke on the last word.

Niebie took a small step backward. "I only picked a flower."

The Oppas spoke, "If I may interject." Both humans turned toward him. "On Aarde you never could've accidentally plucked a bloom filled with a child. Her parents would've been nearby and magicked a duplicate empty bloom into your hands. The thought never even crossed our minds that you took her intentionally."

Mama dropped her face into her hands then raised it, tears drawing lines down her cheeks. "Regardless of intent...we've done a great wrong." Niebie wrapped an arm around her.

"The only reason," Blometje interjected, "any of us are here on Venus...is the Bedrijf."

Mama and Niebie both shushed her.

"We just...must make the best of it," Niebie suggested. "We could...share custody?"

"It does seem like that might be best for Bloemetje," the Oppas agreed.

"Don't you think," Bloemetje's voice piped up, "that Bloemtje might be asked what's best for Bloemtje?" Then, without waiting for a response, she darted between Mama's feet, heading for the dome's wall. As all three adults called after her, she reached it and, turning, ran alongside, seeking out a place where she could think for herself without the constrictions of adults' notions.

But no matter how long or far Bloemetje ran, she was always the same distance from the tulip border. She finally collapsed next to the dome's wall and placed a hand against it. The orange-yellow atmosphere swirled, and Bloemtje thought, I wish I could see just a little further out, not realizing that anytime a fairy makes a wish with all her heart, magic begins.

The atmosphere cleared slightly, and she saw a form. Just a speck in the distance, for it was small like her. Although it was the same colors as the atmosphere, it had a resistant presence. And it began to approach the dome.

As it drew closer, Bloemtje saw that it had a body like

the birds in one of Niebie's books, but dangling beneath were multiple appendages like tentacles. Wings expanded up and behind its body. It had a long neck with a bare globular head and a beak. It hovered in front of her, cocking its head to a variety of angles, with four red eyes gazing at her.

"Zoeker." A voice sounded in Bloemetje's head. The form was speaking, and yet it hadn't actually spoken.

Bloemetje suspected she could simply think her response and did so, "Zoeker?"

"Yes."

"Is that your name? Or your species?"

"Name. Well, name translated from my language into Nederlands. Is that correct? Should I have selected English instead?"

"No, you're correct. All our proper names are in Nederlands." The mere thought of calling someone Seeker instead of Zoeker felt wrong. "How are we able to speak like this?"

"I wished with all my heart. Like how you wished to

see beyond."

"You heard my wish?"

"It was so strong, I bet any magical folk nearby did." Bloemetje looked behind her. Zoeker's beak in a way that she thought might be a laugh. "Don't worry. They're too far away to hear you."

"What are your pronouns?"

Zoeker floated quietly for a moment. "Fae/faer."

"She/her. One of my parents is nonbinary too."

"Among our people, these are not nonbinary pronouns. We don't have nonbinary. We're all the same gender. And this is our gender's pronoun."

"Neat. What is your gender called?"

"We don't call it anything at all since we're all the same."

"Oh, that makes sense."

Zoeker bobbed up and down in a way Bloemetje felt was good-natured. "Would you like to see Lavasteen?"

"Lavasteen?"

"It's the best way to translate our home's name."

Bloemetje nodded. "Lava rock. That's a beautiful name. I'd love to see it."

"Then come out." The dirt at the dome's bottom moved, creating a passageway.

"Won't this hurt the air inside?" asked Bloemetje, thinking of her parents and the fairies.

"I have wished for a magical airlock to protect both atmospheres."

So she lowered herself into the small tunnel, walking through the rocky soil and out the other side. Only when she stood breathing in front of Zoeker did it strike her to wonder at how.

"Because you wanted it so badly," Zoeker responded.

"Why doesn't that work for them?" Bloemetje gestured back at everyone else.

"The humans aren't magic, and the fairies don't wish for it." Fae started to float away. "Come."

Bloemetje followed.

Episode 7

Everything about Lavasteen was the opposite of the dome. It was abruptly rising mountain faces, hard surfaces, cracks with rivers of lava pouring out of them, and a harsh scent that scalded rather than tickled the inside of her nose. Zoeker could swim in the lava, but fae warned Bloemetje that no amount of wishing would make her able to touch that precious part of the planet's life cycle. "Just as your people help your flowers bloom, mine help the rocks form and break down," fae explained. As they contemplated a lava river together, Bloemetje saw how Zoeker's eyes held the same multitudes of shades of red and black, and she felt fae looked at it the way Niebie looked at Mama.

Bloemetje dug into her pocket and pulled out a thimble-sized water bottle Niebie had fashioned for her. She unscrewed the top and took a long drink. Zoeker watched her, then spoke, "My parent went to the Raad when the humans landed and erected the dome."

Bloemetje twisted the lid back on her water bottle. "Are you considered grown yet? I know in some cultures grown children continue to live with their family."

"I'm like you. Almost grown. But not quite."

"When will you be?"

"We don't count only by time alive but also by actions. I hope to be considered fully grown soon."

"I wish my culture did it that way," Bloemetje muttered. Then she resumed the discussion. "Does your parent know you're here? With me?"

Zoeker bobbed up and down, looking at some lava flowing nearby. "No, fae doesn't. My parent told me to stay far away from the area of Invasion. Fae thinks I can't handle it. But I obviously can." Zoeker waved faer tentacles at the two of them.

"Yeah, mine think I can't even handle hanging out inside the dome on my own all day. I can only imagine what they'd think of me being out here." Bloemetje grinned. "Does fae not think you're ready even though you know you are?"

Zoeker looked back at Bloemetje and faer eyes sparkled like obsidians and rubies. "Something like that."

"Our grown-ups aren't so different from each other it seems." She wiped a drip of sweat off her brow. "So what's the Raad?"

"In my culture, everyone is an individual but also part of the larger whole. Like how my tentacles are each their own but also part of me. A group of individuals is a Koppeling. Many Koppelingen gather together into Peulen. The oldest members of the Peulen are designated to the Raad. The Raad ensures all proper parts of the land have a matching fairy. We don't reproduce unless the Raad agrees a region needs a fairy and selects who should birth."

Bloemetje frowned, thinking of Mama. "So someone could really want a baby and not be allowed one?" Then, she thought of herself. "Or not want one and be told to have one?"

Zoeker twisted faer tentacles into pairs then untwisted them. "That's never happened. We all want what the Raad wants. What's best for us all."

"So your parent agreed with the Raad's decision? About the Invasion?"

All four of faer eyes narrowed. "Fae worried about it, but also trusted that it was the most correct choice. As I'm sure you can tell, the Raad decided we shouldn't interfere - at least not right away - even though it pained us all. Much of the damage was already done as soon as the first dome was erected. There was no restoring life to those beings. And the Raad felt we should wait and see your people's behavior over time. But they also wanted fae to keep watch in addition to faes usual duties. My parent wrote a poem about it. I think it's the best record we have of your people's invasion. Would you like to hear?"

A part of Bloemetje resisted hearing how her people had hurt Zoeker's. But another part of her, the seed of

God's light within her that Mama often spoke about to her at bedtime, told her she should listen. "I'd be honored if you shared it."

So Zoeker straightened out faer body and spoke. "A Fairy's Responsibility by Baseren.

When the rocks screamed,
I answered their call too late.

A spaceship's weight already
Crushed the life-cycle out of them.

They trembled a rattling death-knell,
And tears flowed from my four red eyes.

My tentacles tingled to their tips, all six reaching
For the lava retreating beneath the slaughtered rocks.

With a whir and a whoosh their exit was cut off,
By a dome the size of a great boulder appearing.

My body elongated, and two more eyes sprouted,
As the wish for retribution began to form in my body.

'Parent, what's happening?' asked my child beside me,
And I knew I must demonstrate acting instead of reacting.

I buried my magic-boosting eyes behind quartz-colored skin.
'We must calmly inform the Raad immediately,' I answered.

We soared to their semi-circle fronting the sheer-sided cliff
But hovered back with their short-sighted pacifist orders.

'As fairies we have the responsibility
To ensure balance in the life cycle.

You will watch and wait to determine
If these intend greater destruction.

Perhaps it's like when some rocks die

To allow the lava to come through.'

Yet as I commenced monitoring,
I quivered with my knowing

This was an invasion
Of Lavasteen."

Episode 8

Tears welled in Bloemetje's eyes when Zoeker finished reciting faer parent's poem. "You were there too? When my people arrived?"

"Yes."

"I'm so sorry. I can only imagine how that must have felt."

Zoeker bobbed up and down in silence.

Bloemetje rubbed her eyes, wiping the tears away. "So you being here...is that going against the Raad?"

"I don't think so. I was at the meeting with them too, you know, since I also witnessed the arrival. They said 'wait and see.' I think meeting and talking with you is a type of waiting and seeing."

Bloemetje nodded. "Parents can be overprotective."

"And wrong."

Bloemetje giggled. "Yes, and wrong." But then her

laughter faded. "My parents told me Aarde, our planet, was dying. The Bedrijf is trying to make a new place for humans to live."

"Your Bedrijf isn't simply trying to find refuge. Why is it driving your parents and their colleagues to work nearly constantly preparing to make more domes when what they have is enough to support those already here?"

"I think they're planning to bring more humans here…"

"At the cost of death to ever more of our indigenous life. Every dome destroys the whole cycle of lava and rock and soil where it sits. Replaced by your own."

Bloemetje didn't want this to be true, because of what it would mean about her parents, so she protested, in spite of what she had heard in Zoeker's parent's poem. "Can rocks really die? Or lava? They're not alive like plants."

"Oh, they're alive." At this a collection of small rocks gathered into a pile next to Zoeker.

"You're using magic."

"I'm not."

"Then I would have seen them move before."

"How much can you see outside your dome? And how much would you move if aliens that were murdering your neighbors were watching you?"

"My parents aren't murderers."

Zoeker squished back down together into a more ball-like shape and reached one tentacle toward her. "I'm not saying it's intentional. But it's still murder. My people cannot let it continue. And any good people among your own should want to right the wrong as best they can."

Bloemetje gazed at the rocks then at Zoeker. She couldn't deny what was right in front of her, even as bile rose in the back of her throat at the new knowledge. Now she understood how Niebie and Mama must have felt mere hours ago. "I'm sorry. You're correct, of course....But how can my people right it?" Her head felt overly full. A pain stabbed behind her eyes. This was all too much for a fifteen day old fairy like herself to handle.

A fairy who just learned she even is one. With only a small amount of knowledge of her own people and culture.

All she had wanted today was the freedom to roam and breathe among the plants she loved without being constantly hidden and shushed. She sat on the hard soil beneath her and took slow, deep breaths. Gradually the pain in her head abated. She looked up at Zoeker. "My parents' hearts would break if they knew they were killing living creatures. And my fairies said they're only here because the Bedrijf brought the tulips. I don't know much about Aarde but it confuses me how terraforming can work here and not there. It seems to me that we should go back and terraform there." She stood up, balling her hands into fists at her sides.

Zoeker squished faer body together and apart, shortening and elongating. "Yes. It won't bring back those who lived where your dome is but at least it will prevent more deaths."

"The Bedrijf has power over my people, though. It

frightens my parents. I'm not sure if…" She looked into the distance then back at Zoeker, a new determination in her eye. "But I'll speak with them tonight. Can I meet you again tomorrow?"

"Yes."

"And Zoeker…thank you. To you and your people. For giving us a chance even when we've harmed you."

Fae bobbed up and down in acknowledgement, "We prefer to act rather than react," Zoeker echoed the lesson from faer parent without realizing fae was doing so. Then, fae guided Bloemetje back to the dome. She went down into the tunnel and returned inside. She knew her parents would just be finishing up their workday. Much as Bloemetje liked the idea of the fairy festival to welcome her back, she couldn't celebrate after what she'd just learned. So she found her parents' lunchbox and climbed inside.

Episode 9

Bloemetje sat squirreled away inside the family lunchbox, listening to her parents' footsteps as they walked home. It felt like Niebie's way of carrying the lunchbox - at a slight jaunt away from their body rather than in Mama's tight grasp. The family's front door squeaked as it opened then again as it closed. Bloemetje felt a slight shift followed by solidity as Niebie set the lunchbox down on the table. A chair scraped against the floor when one of her parents sat. She didn't want to eavesdrop, so she called out, "Niebie? Mama? I'm here."

Mama gasped as the chair moved once again, and the lunchbox's top opened, revealing Niebie standing over her, their mouth gaping, with Mama just behind them, her eyes shining. Niebie's lips tightened into a line before they spoke, "How could you run off like that?"

"You gave us such a fright," Mama added.

Bloemetje wanted to say something cutting and mean back to them. But thoughts of Zoeker's parent's admonition to act rather than react ran through her head, and she held her tongue. Just as Niebie was beginning a rant about how she could have been killed, Mama placed a hand on their arm, bringing silence to the hut. Then Mama spoke. "You frightened us so, Bloemetje. But you are…growing up. And this is a difficult situation. We want you to feel that you can speak to…no, speak with us."

"Thank you," Bloemetje said. "Can you help me out of here first?"

Niebie reached in a hand for her while Mama got Bloemetje's chair from the cupboard, placing it on the table near her. Bloemetje chose to stand near it, grasping its back with a hand for solidity. Then she told them all about Zoeker and faer people. Mama collapsed onto a chair partway through her tale. By the time she was done, Niebie was staring out the window.

The three of them communed together in silence for a

time. Finally, Niebie spoke, "This is horrible. But we can't return."

Bloemetje looked back and forth between the two of them. "Why not?"

"Terraforming won't work fast enough on Aarde."

"That's why we have to colonize." Mama added.

"I don't understand."

Niebie turned from the window. "It's a slow process. The only reason it's working here is we've never exceeded the population the dome can handle. Aarde isn't like that. There are billions of people. Exhausted land. Unbreathable air. Trying to terraform there…"

Mama picked up a bowl and thimble from the table and brought them to the sink. "Imagine this water was running." She didn't turn it on as the Bedrijf regulated water usage. "The bowl is full and overflowing. And I'm trying to stop it by removing a thimbleful of water at a time. That's what terraforming on Aarde is like."

Tightness crept across Bloemetje's chest.

"So you see," Niebie added, "the only way to save

humanity as a species, to make things better, is to try someplace else."

"The Bedrijf thought they chose an uninhabited planet. And you must admit, Bloemetje, it's not like there are people here," Mama stated.

"Do I not count as a person to you?" Bloemetje demanded.

Both of her parents insisted that of course she did.

"Zoeker isn't any different from me. And fae can't live without the rocks, soil, and lava. They're all alive. Just like our plants. Who are you to say who counts as a person? You ruin our planet, fly here, destroy the living beings here, steal me, and then say it's all just to save yourselves?"

"We didn't steal you…" Mama protested.

"You did. Even if you didn't mean to."

Niebie cringed at that, and tears entered Mama's eyes. Bloemetje bit her lip but pressed on. "Don't you see how this is destroying you two as well? Because I do. Neither of you have joy. At least the fairies still manage some, even while struggling with the pathetic imitation of a society the Bedrijf left them with. What do you have?"

"Each other," Niebie answered.

"And you," Mama added.

"That's more than those who lived where the dome is now will ever have again. But it's also not enough. I've never liked the Bedrijf. But I couldn't imagine another way. Meeting the fairies and Zoeker, hearing about other ways....it made me think we can do something different than what we have now. Something that makes everyone joyful. That steers us all the right way."

"There's companies on Aarde too," Mama protested.

"Isn't working to fix Aarde better than stealing someone else's world? And losing our own goodness in the process?"

"Bloemetje." Niebie approached her, bending down a little so they were at eye-level with each other. "To return to Aarde with nothing new to suggest to fix things....At best they might let us rejoin them, resume a half-life of oxygen tanks and imitation food. At worst, they might kill us for coming back."

"And we could never afford oxygen tanks without the Bedrijf's support," Mama's voice floated to them from the sink.

The phrase something new tickled at Bloemetje's mind. "When you say something new...you mean what exactly?"

"Some better way to fix Aarde," Niebie answered.

"Ok, well, let's all try to think of something."

"Aarde's best scientists couldn't think of anything. What makes you think we can?" Niebie asked.

"Oh, let her try. What could it hurt," Mama sighed, still staring down into the sink, not looking at either of them.

They all went to bed, but Bloemetje laid awake thinking.

Episode 10

Bloemetje stayed up most of the night trying to figure out a faster way to fix Aarde. She should have woken up groggy and maybe even a little depressed after the day she'd had before, but with the power of youth she woke refreshed. She rolled over in bed and bumped into her tiny notebook Niebie had fashioned for her. There was the note she jotted down late at night so she wouldn't forget. A potential solution to their problems. She leaped out of bed and gave a knock on the human-sized bowl her parents set up every night to give everyone some privacy. Her parents moaned in response.

"Good morning! Hurry, we need to start the day."

"Our alarm hasn't gone off yet," protested Niebie.

"Oh," Bloemetje glanced at the window. Its curtain was drawn but light peeked around the sides anyway. "But the new day is here, is it not?"

There was rustling on the other side of the bowl as Mama looked at her phone. "It indeed is here," she confirmed, then quieter to Niebie, "The alarm is about to go off anyway."

Bloemetje heard her parents getting up and decided now was the time to assert her plans. "I need to speak with the flower fairies. Today."

Niebie moved the bowl aside and looked down at her. "Of course. It's important to us that you get to know your people."

The water ran briefly as Mama filled the kettle for morning tea. She called over, "We'll leave our lunchbox near the tulips. Just be sure to be back before our shift is over."

Bloemetje readily agreed. And so, after breakfast together, her parents walked to the field and set down the lunchbox holding Bloemetje near the tulips. Niebie reached a hand in for Bloemetje and gently placed her on the ground. They couldn't say anything, but Bloemetje felt the fond farewell anyway. She gazed at Niebie's and

Mama's departing backs then turned, startling slightly as there, right behind her, stood the Oppas. "I suspected you might show back up today."

"I'm sorry I missed the festival….and for any worry I may have caused."

The Oppas waved his hand. "I suspect you've already had this conversation with your parents. No need to repeat it." He turned and began to walk among the tulips. She darted after him, slowing to match his pace when she reached his side. "Thank you. That's true. But there's something else going on I need to speak with you about. It's urgent."

"Alright. You can tell me when we get to my tulip."

Bloemetje was able to sense when an elder wanted silence and so bit her tongue until they arrived at a bright yellow tulip that he gazed upon fondly for a moment. Then he sighed and sat. "So. Tell me what's going on, young one."

She told him of Zoeker, faer people, and what her parents said the night before. A vertical line appeared in his forehead when she began her tale and gradually deepened as she finished it. They sat in silence together for a moment. Then Bloemetje broke it with the question that she hoped would lead into discussing the possible solution she'd thought of the night before. "Do you understand why it's such a problem to terraform Aarde?"

He nodded. "Humans rely on plants to clean the air, but they can't keep up with the rate of degradation from humanity's advances."

"My parents said it was overpopulation."

"Hmm...selfish shortsightedness would be a more accurate description. Something the companies encourage. Once humans added them to the equation, pollution came. The more industrialized a society, the greater a negative impact on the planet. Currently all of Aarde is companies but once there were parts that lived more like us flower fairies. They had as many children as they wished but because they didn't live solely for consumption it took many of their people to equal the pollution caused by just one in company areas." The Oppas rubbed his chin. "The Bedrijf thinks it can prevent that from happening again here by regulating not just population but additional things like energy production and water usage. They bring air into this dome and then release it out into a newly forming one. Once it's suitable enough to support plants, they'll plant them there and continue. Who's to say if it'll work long-term."

"You must have an opinion on that."

He quirked an eyebrow then sighed. "Indeed, I do. Their plan is to charge humans from Aarde large sums to be brought here to completed domes. Once they start to see the money from that…I think the Bedrijf's greediness will outweigh their foresight."

"And ruin this planet too?"

The Oppas shrugged. "Maybe."

Episode 11

Bloemetje bit her lip as Oppas's statement brought a vision of the domes expanding across Venus's entire landscape then turning into places uninhabitable for humans anyway to her. She subconsciously shook her head slightly. "How do you know all this?" she asked him. "It's a lot of high-level detail about Bedrijf for a small fairy."

"You'd be amazed how much the leidinggevenden discuss here where they think no one is listening. In fact," he added, "I'd say fairies tend to know a lot about the human world. Humans tend to ignore anything smaller than them."

Bloemetje nodded. "Let me see if I have it right. Humans rely on plants to clean the air. Here the plants can clean it at a pace that keeps their pollution from making the atmosphere unlivable. But in order for humans to successfully live on Aarde, they need a plant that can change its atmosphere more quickly than any plants currently can. To outpace the rate at which they hurt it themselves."

"That or to create less pollution. But we know from experience it's very unlikely they'll ever pollute less. And, unfortunately, no plant that can keep up with the rate of pollution on Aarde exists."

"Not yet anyway."

He quirked an eyebrow at her. "What are you thinking, young one?

She leaned in toward him. "Well, we are fairies, aren't we? And fairies have both magic...and flowers. Which are a plant."

"....we do."

"So...is there a tulip bulb I can have?"

He cupped an elbow with one hand and tapped his lips with the other. Bloemetje thought she might have to ask him again, but then he spoke, "The one from your birth is rightfully yours." A warmth flooded Bloemetje's chest and spread to a beaming smile on her face. The Oppas smiled back at her and continued. "I'll take you to it."

So he guided her along the rows of flowers to her bulb. "How do we go about digging it up?" she asked.

"This will help," a voice chimed in from nearby. Bloemetje turned and saw a flower fairy of her generation holding a fairy-sized shovel. "I'm Rineke, she/her," she tapped her chest. She was a bit taller than Bloemetje with hair that expanded out around her head. Her height and hair, combined with the sturdiness of her limbs, reminded Bloemetje of one of Aarde's majestic trees in Niebie's nature programs.

"I'm Bloemetje."

Rineke laughed a sound full of the richness and warmth of a cup of cocoa. "I know. We all do."

Bloemetje blushed. "Oh, of course."

"Why don't I let you two young ones dig up the bulb," the Oppas sighed and sat down nearby.

Rineke moved forward as if to dig.

"I should," Bloemetje said, "it's my bulb."

"We'll take turns. That's what communities do."

Bloemetje wanted to do it entirely herself but she had to admit Rineke was correct. Solitary-mindedness was exactly the sort of behavior the Bedrijf would want. So she acquiesced. "Yes, it is. Thank you."

Rineke began digging. "So why weren't you at the festival last night? We were all looking forward to getting to know you."

Bloemetje had been watching the spot in the dirt where Rineke was digging, but this question led her to look up. "Oh I very much wanted to meet you all as well. I hadn't thought about how my not coming might come across to you...."

"You'd only been thinking about what the elders would think." It was a statement, not a question or an accusation.

"Yes." Rineke paused in her digging and Bloemetje stepped forward, holding out her hand for the shovel. Rineke handed it to her and took a sip of water from a bottle hanging at her waist. Bloemetje started digging. "It was thoughtless of me, and I do apologize."

"I accept. And I'm sure the others will as well."

"May I tell you why I missed it? Not as an excuse. Just as information."

Rineke held out the water bottle to her, and she exchanged the shovel for it, allowing Rineke to take a turn again. "Of course. I'm interested to know."

So Bloemetje told her about Zoeker, faer people, and her own plan to put the humans and fairies living in the colony on a different course of action, while the Oppas began snoring from his resting place on the ground nearby.

Episode 12

But Rineke wasn't as interested in the big picture of all of their futures as Bloemetje was expecting. She zeroed in on a different aspect of the story entirely, asking as the two of them again swapped water for shovel, with Rineke taking the water and Bloemetje the shovel, "You have a thing for this Zoeker, don't you?"

"I do not."

"You're blushing!"

Bloemetje's heart raced. "It's flushed from the digging."

"Be careful, we're close to it now. You might want to switch to your hands."

Bloemetje put the shovel down and knelt, digging into the soft, rich soil with her bare hands, the soil pushing up under her fingernails as she felt for her birthright.

Rineke leaned over beside her, inspecting her progress.

"Ok, so you don't have a thing for faer. You do have some sort of feelings, though, right?"

Bloemetje looked up at Rineke. She couldn't lie in the face of a newly forming friendship. "Of course I have some feelings. Zoeker is…incredible. I feel different when I'm with faer. Like…it's not that I don't already want to be a good person. I do. It's just that, when I'm with faer, it feels…like something I also want to do because of faer. Fae brings out the best in me. I don't know. I haven't met very many people in my life, but something about us together feels…special." Bloemetje's fingers brushed against something solid in the dirt. A part of her knew instantly it was her bulb. She felt forward with her fingertips. Once she had one hand on each side of the bulb, she tugged, not thinking about how a small person like herself could possibly lift such a large object. But lift it she did, pulling it up to the light. Rineke and Bloemetje gazed at it together.

"So why are you saying you don't have a thing for Zoeker?"

"Because I don't..." Bloemetje hesitated.

"I was there when you told the Koinigin that you don't want babies. Do you think that means you can't have romantic feelings? That you can't have a beloved?"

Bloemetje, for the first time in days, lost her voice. She nodded.

"It absolutely does not mean that."

"It doesn't?"

Rineke laughed again, and the gentle sound washed over Bloemetje, soothing an ache in her heart she didn't know she had. "Of course it doesn't. Romance doesn't automatically mean that babies must come along with it. Look at your parents. And romance doesn't necessarily come alongside babies either. I've heard of fairies who make a baby who are not beloveds."

"You have?"

"Yes." Rineke nodded at the Oppas. "He told me about them."

"I wonder why he knows so much about different fairies and yet the Koningin still seems surprised."

"Some people seem to have the weakness of trying to hold onto things the way they think they should be rather than letting them be as they are. It seems that not everyone learns to let go by the time they're an elder."

Bloemetje stood. "You're certainly wise for a fairy my age."

"I'm told I'm a lot like my fathers in that way."

"An old soul?"

"A nosy one always asking questions." Rineke smiled. "You can let go now," she added.

"Of my preconceived notions?"

She laughed. "Yes, but also of your bulb."

"It'll fall."

"You can float it with your magic. Just wish it to be so."

So Bloemetje let go of the bulb, wishing for it to float, and it did, bobbing up and down in front of her like Zoeker when fae was deep in thought. "If only knowing what to do with romantic feelings was as easy as this."

"I'm not sure what romantic feelings you young ones

are discussing," came the Oppas's voice from behind them, giving them both a small start, "but my advice is to tell the person how you feel as soon as you can." He came up beside Bloemetje and rested a hand on her shoulder. "Life is short."

"Thank you, elder," Bloemetje and Rineke murmured. Then, after saying her farewells, Bloemetje turned and power walked off toward the small passageway out of the dome to meet Zoeker. It was time for the next phase of her plan. And maybe for a small addition to it as well.

Episode 13

As Bloemetje made her way across Lavasteen's expanse, floating her bulb in front of her, she sought the slight solidity in the atmosphere that would indicate Zoeker's presence. She did not have to look for long, for soon she saw a part of the creamsicle-like clouds that appeared to be more solid. The instant she spotted this area, it twirled and shot up into the sky. Not an it at all, then, but rather a fae - Zoeker. Bloemetje's heart soared with faer, so much that she almost checked to see if it had burst out of her chest to join faer. But all of her, save for her birthright bulb, remained on the ground.

She came to a stop just below where Zoeker bobbed, weaved, and twirled above. The movements reminded her of the one time Niebie cajoled Mama to dance with them in the family's hut, and all Bloemetje wanted was to move in this way with Zoeker. Her body started to float up in response to this wish but Zoeker sped down to her, bobbing and weaving around her as Bloemetje's feet settled back on the ground. Zoeker came to a stop in front of her and extended four tentacles toward her. "You returned."

Bloemetje reached out with her own two arms and lightly squeezed the tips of two of Zoeker's tentacles then released them. She nodded. "Did you think I wouldn't?"

Zoeker squished down into a tight ball. "I was harsh with you…"

"No," Bloemetje interrupted, "you were honest and justly angry about a deep wrong being done to you and your people. Being perpetrated by my people…and me."

"Not intentionally."

"No, but my presence here is part of the problem, isn't it?"

Zoeker returned to faer usual shape and bobbed gently up and down, not unlike Bloemetje's bulb just beside them. Fae twisted faer tentacles into pairs then released them. "Your presence here is both a beautiful miracle… and a terrible wrong."

"Yes,…that's how I feel too. Now that I've been outside the dome, I love Lavasteen for just how it is naturally. But it would be wrong for me to stay." She clenched and unclenched her fists, mirroring Zoeker without realizing it. "So, that's why I've come up with a plan. To get all of us back to Aarde."

"What plan is that?" Zoeker asked.

So Bloemetje told fae the shape of the idea that formed in her head late the night before and solidified further as she spoke with the Oppas. When she finished, they sat together, gazing at her bulb. Then Zoeker spoke, "So you want to change this so it will do what it does naturally. Only more and faster?"

Bloemetje inhaled and held her breath slightly, feeling how hearing someone else describe the plan made it feel fully real for the first time. She nodded. "If it works we can do it to all the rest. Then the humans can take us fairies and our bulbs back to Aarde so we can begin fixing it."

Zoeker's eyes glowed brighter. "I'm excited to do this with you."

Bloemetje blushed. "Me too." She looked away, unable to say the next part while looking at faer. "I like doing things with you." Then a soft warmth accentuated by gentle suckers covered her hand. She looked down at where Zoeker's tentacle rested on her hand and added softly, "My feelings for you are..." but the right word escaped her.

Thankfully, Zoeker finished the sentence for her. "Special?"

Bloemetje could only nod.

"So are mine for you." Zoeker made a burbling sound that reminded Bloemetje of a sigh. The first truly audible sound she'd ever heard from faer.

A desire to comfort fae overcame her own melancholy at experiencing these feelings with a person in a place she could not remain. "Perhaps God wants us to see that our people meeting didn't have to be full of pain and death. It could have been different. If only my people had behaved differently."

"Yes. Maybe if you tell the next generation about this… about us…they will figure out a way for our people to meet in a way of mutual respect and trust, not colonization. And then our people could become allies, friends,…maybe even some can become something more." Zoeker responded. Bloemetje ever so gently leaned her head against the side of faer body. Fae felt warm and soft against her cheek, like a fuzzy blanket.

They sat in silence together for a moment. Then Bloemetje asked, "Do you think we can make my plan work?"

"Yes. I think we can." Zoeker's suckers sucked lightly at the back of her hand then fae removed faer tentacle and turned to some of the small rocks nearby. Bloemetje sat back up fully to give fae room. The rocks moved to rest on top of the bulb like a hiker's cairn. Lava came up from the ground, forming a tiny fiery circular creek around it. Zoeker moved to the other side of the set-up and extended two tentacles across. Bloemetje put out her hands, wrapping her fingers around the silky smoothness as Zoeker wrapped part of faer tentacles up around her wrists. Together, without needing to pre-plan, they made the same wish.

God of Lavasteen and of Aarde. Create a plant in this bulb that will set right Aarde's wrongs. Save Lavasteen. Save Aarde.

Bloemetje found herself holding her breath as, together, they waited to see what would happen.

Episode 14

Just as Bloemetje thought she must surely admit defeat and cease holding her breath, the bulb crackled and popped, changing. No longer did it look like an unpeeled white onion with a brown wrapper. The brown changed to black the same as the lava rocks around them. And the part extending up out of the wrapper that used to be white was the red of flowing lava.

"Well, something happened," Bloemetje whispered as they released the grasp they had on each other.

"How long does it take plants to grow?" Zoeker asked.

"Too long."

"Let's speed it up then so we can see." Zoeker extended faer tentacles again. Bloemetje hesitated. "My elders say tulips only bloom if fairies who are each other's beloveds make a baby grow inside."

Zoeker steadied in the air and floated faer tentacles

outward around fae like beams of light from the sun. "Well, we're halfway there."

"Does that mean...?" Bloemetje couldn't bear to look at faer as she asked the question.

"Yes, Bloemetje. I feel for you as one feels for a beloved."

Bloemetje beamed and felt such a strong wish to be near Zoeker that she started to lift off the ground. "I feel that way about you too."

Zoeker swooped down to her and twirled. Bloemetje giggled and came back to rest on the ground. Zoeker stopped twirling and bobbed happily up and down. A warmth spread in Bloemetje's mind that felt like a telepathic smile from Zoeker.

Bloemetje was afraid to say more and break the beauty of the moment, but she knew she must. "But, Zoeker, I don't want a baby."

"This kind of liking doesn't have to go hand-in-hand with making babies. It doesn't for my people."

"It doesn't?"

"No. Wishing to be a parent and loving someone are completely separate. If I was to decide I was ready to be a parent, I would approach my Koppeling and make my wishes known. If the Koppeling supported me, they would inform the Peul. If the Peul supported me, they would simply ask the Raad if there's a plot of land available for another individual in the near future. Then it would be so. We want to ensure that there is land in need of a fairy before we make more."

Bloemetje thought of Mama. "Are people who want a baby told no?"

"Only wait. Never no. Sometimes it's that we need a few more elders to pass on first. Sometimes it's that the individual needs some training before fae is ready."

Bloemetje nodded. "Thank you for sharing that with me." She looked once again at the bulb. "I'm glad there's precedent with your people but...what if we can't make the flower bloom without a baby?"

The whooshing and crackling of the lava flowing nearby filled what otherwise would have been silence as they both thought on the concerning question. Then, Zoeker spoke. "Maybe it's not the baby that makes the bloom but, rather, beloveds gathering nearby and wishing for it. I mean no disrespect to your elders and their wisdom. But perhaps it's just that it's uncommon among your flower fairies...yet not impossible. "

Bloemetje thought about how many different combinations of beloved fairies could make a flower bloom. The only thing they all had in common was wishing for both the bloom and the baby. "Perhaps you're right about that. It certainly can't hurt for us to try." She reached out her hands toward Zoeker.

Fae extended faer tentacles in return and clasped her as before. Together they thought grow, grow, grow. Bloemetje thought (if anything happened at all) that they would have a long wait, longer than before, but almost immediately a shoot exploded out of the bulb and reached upward. Bloemetje and Zoeker yelped and released each other. The rocks on top of the cairn scuttled away. The lava backed up, giving the flower room. It shot roots down into the hard soil. The stem and leaves were green, as expected. But the flower blooming out of it was lava red, streaked in black stripes that matched that of cooled lava rock. Bloemetje darted to it and glanced inside. She was relieved to find no fairy baby. "We did it," she said to Zoeker, looking up at faer face, and when she did, she saw the atmosphere around the flower changing in color and density, fading away from the orange hues to invisibility like inside the domes. "It's working!"

"Too well," Zoeker responded. "Get it back inside before it terraforms here."

Bloemetje reached for one of faer tentacles and gave it a squeeze. Then she grabbed the flower and dashed away.

Episode 15

The moment Bloemetje arrived back in the dome, she went right to the tulips, seeking her fairies. She realized she didn't know where they lived. Surely it couldn't be in the flowers themselves? Blooms don't last forever. She hesitated, her new flower floating just off the ground, attempting to blend in with the rest.

"Bloemetje," Rineke's voice called out to her. Bloemetje turned and, spotting her friend, waved. "You were successful," Rineke cried as she walked up next to her, her face taking on a look of awe.

"It seems so. Will you take me to the Koningin and the Oppas?"

"Of course, they should be at home taking their afternoon rest right about now." Rineke led her to a rock next to what seemed to Bloemetje to be the plainest tulip of them all. "This isn't really a rock. It's a glamor hiding the entrance to our homes underground." Rineke waved her hand and, indeed, the rock vanished before Bloemetje's eyes, revealing a doorway. "But your flower won't fit underground, so I'll go down and get them."

Bloemetje said her thanks and shifted from foot to foot while she waited. Just a few moments later, the door opened again, and Rineke emerged, followed by the Koningin and the Oppas.

The Koningin held a stern expression on her face, while the Oppas beside her barely concealed a smile behind his hand. "Bloemetje," the Koningin spoke, "What have you here?" she gestured at the flower.

"I call it Cadeau van Lavasteen," she responded.

"Gift of Lava Rock. Why?" The Koningin asked.

Bloemetje explained that Lavasteen was the best translation of the planet's true name. Then she described meeting Zoeker and who fae was. What fae told her. How they worked together to make this hybrid. And how together they could transform all the bulbs this way so when it was time for the flower fairies to wish for blooms and babies, they could terraform Aarde.

"The Bedrijf will never allow it," the Koningin insisted.

"You're right. But we won't give it a choice."

The Koningin raised an eyebrow. "Fairies haven't interfered in human ways in a very long time, my dear."

"Maybe we should have. Maybe that's part of what caused the imbalance on Aarde. Maybe we're supposed to help steer them back the right way when needed."

The Koningin gazed at the Cadeau van Lavasteen for a few moments. Bloemetje waited, barely breathing. Finally, the Koningin spoke. "Maybe so." She turned to the Oppas and dipped her head to him. "But only if you agree, my dear and respected friend."

He lowered his head to her in return. "Indeed I do."

"Yes!" Bloemetje cried as she jumped up and down gleefully like the sixteen day old fairy she was.

"You do still need to speak with your parents, my dear," the Koningin called to her with a smile. Then more firmly, "We need as many humans on our side as possible."

"Yes, of course, you're right, ma'am," she responded.

"And any humans that won't become our comrades, I can wish to sleep a deep sleep until we're safely off the planet," the Koningin added.

So Bloemetje floated the Cadeau van Lavasteen with her to the pepper plants and, using her newly found skill, floated both herself and the flower into her parents' lunchbox. It was nearly the end of the workday, and she had to wait less than an hour before the top lifted, revealing Niebie's face. They gave her a wink, then their eyes widened as they spotted the tulip. But they closed the top without saying a word and carried her home. After the door closed, and she felt the lunchbox come to rest on the table, she opened the top herself with her own fairy wish and floated out alongside the tulip. Niebie was so taken with the hybrid that they didn't notice their own daughter flying. They stared at the hybrid. "Wow! It's incredible." They reached a fingertip toward it, then withdrew. "What is it?"

So Bloemetje explained.

"I can feel it cleaning," Mama declared as she finished.

"The Bedrijf will never agree to returning to Aarde, though," Niebie added.

"Don't ask them, then." Bloemetje meant it to sound like a suggestion, but it came out more like an order.

Mama walked up to Niebie, placing her hand on their arm. "She's right. I keep thinking about how you plucking that flower was both right and wrong. On Aarde it would've simply been a lovely gesture for me when I wasn't well. The only reason it was wrong at all was because we're here. We don't belong here. And if we keep obeying the Bedrijf we're just going to keep doing things that are wrong. At their orders. But wrong nonetheless."

Niebie nodded. "Ever since you told us about it, Bloemetje, I haven't been able to stop thinking about all the Lavasteen life we've been killing while we're here. It makes me feel sick. But I know if we tell the Bedrijf they won't care."

"We need to start doing things because we know

they're right. Not because the Bedrijf says so," Mama said.

Niebie nodded and squeezed her hand. "And we need to give our colleagues the chance to make their own decision with the same knowledge we now have. We'll spread the word tonight. How long do you need?"

"I can't imagine it will take more than a few hours to transform them all."

"Well, I think it would be best to give yourselves a full day to achieve such a task. Just in case. Besides, we'll need that time to speak with our colleagues to see who will become our comrades," Mama responded.

"What of those who won't?" Niebie asked.

"The Koningin can put them to sleep so they can't interfere until we've already left," Bloemetje suggested.

Both of her parents nodded. "That should work. So we'll plan to take over the ship the morning after tomorrow."

Bloemetje opened her mouth to protest but Mama held her hand up. "Plus, I think you deserve as much time with Zoeker as we can reasonably manage. To say farewell."

Bloemetje's feet touched the table as the full realization hit her. If their plan worked, tomorrow would be the last time she ever saw fae. "You're right, Mama," she murmured.

Niebie bent over the table. "Putting what's right first even when it hurts...it's very wise, Bloemetje."

"Yes, I'm amazed at what a wise person you're growing into," Mama added.

And Bloemetje found the ache in her heart easing slightly as she leaned into Niebie's offered hand, hugging it.

Episode 16

The next morning, Mama and Niebie once again slipped Bloemetje to the flower fairies. "Before we gather the bulbs, Mama needs to distract the humans," Bloemetje told her people. They all turned to watch as Mama among the saplings in the middle of the dome, gesticulating. Soon enough, all the human workers trickled over to her.

"Alright, time to dig," Bloemetje said.

But Oppas held up a hand. "There's not time for manual digging. Children, everyone close your eyes and wish with all your might for your bulb to come to you."

Bloemetje could hardly believe she hadn't thought of this herself. "Of course, you're right, Oppas, this is a much better plan."

"Thank you, my dear, but no time to talk. Wish, everyone."

And so, the entire generation of flower fairies bowed their heads, closed their eyes, and wished. With a sound like a boom to the fairies but just a faint rumble to the humans who were otherwise distracted by fears about failing saplings, all the bulbs came up out of the ground and hovered near their respective fairy.

"You're all amazing," Bloemetje praised.

"Time to go," the Koningin said. So Bloemetje wished for the bulbs to follow her, and they did, staying low to the ground, over to the hole in the dome. She sent them out one at a time, taking a few glances back, amazed at how the humans remained distracted by what Mama was saying to them about the saplings. She shook her head, confident now that when Mama and Niebie switched to speaking with their colleagues about becoming comrades in the plan that more might agree than she'd initially dared to hope would.

She exhaled then scrambled through the hole after the bulbs, gathering them around her like a flock of birds. Floating herself just off the ground beside them, she flew herself and the bulbs out to what she now thought of as her and Zoeker's usual place. Just as she hoped, fae waited for her there. She set herself down on the ground, bringing the bulbs to rest around her, while Zoeker squished down then spun in the air. "They said yes."

"They did." Bloemetje beamed. "I hope you don't mind…I named our hybrid. We can change the name if you don't like it."

"We choose our own names, so naming it never even crossed my mind. I'm sure I'll like the name you gave it. What is it?"

"Cadeau van Lavasteen."

"It's beautiful. Just like your nature."

Bloemetje blushed. "Thank you. Now, we should get to work. We have a lot to do."

And so, one by one, over the course of that day, they transformed the bulbs into hybrids, just as they did the day before. This time, though, they simply wished for the transformation, not performing the second wish for a bloom. As she and Zoeker stood surveying their handiwork, Bloemetje spoke, "My parents and their comrades plan to take over the ship and return to Aarde tomorrow. They'll abandon anyone not on their side here. Those left behind will continue terraforming."

Zoeker lengthened, sprouting two additional eyes, and all six grew larger and brighter. "My people will deal with whoever is left." Seeing Zoeker at faer most threatening caused a shudder to go through her. Zoeker squished back down to faer previous form and returned to faer usual four eyes. "Don't be frightened, beloved."

"No, you have the right to be upset. And your people have the right to justice. I'm just grateful you were willing to help us...even though we came here."

"You yourself weren't even fully formed yet."

"Still." She extended a hand, and Zoeker clasped it with three tentacles.

"May you have success."

"And you."

Tears pooled in the corners of Bloemetje's eyes. "I'll miss you."

"And I you." Streams of lava red dripped out of all four of faer eyes. "I'll never forget you."

"Nor I you." Bloemetje brushed a tear from her own eye then leaned her head forward and into Zoeker's soft side. "Let's spend the next hour pretending like we have a lifetime together. I want to know what that feels like."

And so Bloemetje and Zoeker spent the next hour together. First they walked along the lava river. Then they laid on their backs on top of a tall butte, pointing out patterns in the atmosphere to each other while Bloemetje's hand and three of Zoeker's tentacles intertwined. Leaving the butte, they flew circles around each other in the air. "You taught me how to fly, Zoeker," Bloemetje called between her giggles.

"And you taught me this," Zoeker called back then paused, releasing a burble from faer beak. Fae was giggling too.

Finally they came back to the collection of bulbs and settled down next to them. Bloemetje on the ground, and Zoeker hovering just above the ground next to her.

Zoeker leaned down and placed the space above faer eyes at Bloemetje's forehead. "I love you," fae spoke into Bloemetje's mind.

And, one last time, Bloemetje spoke back into faers. "And I love you." Then, they released each other, and Bloemetje turned and walked back across the rocky expanse with the bulbs floating behind her.

The next morning, when the leidinggevenden reached the garden, no crew of workers was to be found. Slightly less than half were asleep and slightly more than half were approaching the airlock connecting the dome with the ship. The two comrades guarding the ship, who had both agreed to the plan, opened the airlock. Mama and Niebie along with the Koningin, the Oppas, and, of course, Bloemetje, had been designated leadership positions, at least for the time, by their comrades. So Mama got to be the one to turn around and signal to the hidden fairies with a wave. The fairies, floating the tulip bulbs with them, came to the ship. Bloemetje took up the rear. She lingered at the airlock, gazing through the dome to Lavasteen's atmosphere. But no part of it solidified into Zoeker's form. She told herself she shouldn't have expected it to. How would fae know the exact moment they were leaving? But disappointment sunk like a rock in her belly anyway as she turned and finished walking through the airlock onto the ship.

Episode 17

Mama and Niebie stood waiting for her just inside the ship's door. Bloemetjje looked around the cold metal hall. "Wow, so this is how we got here, huh?"

"Yes, and it's how we'll get home." Mama knelt down, bringing herself closer to Bloemetje. "On the flight here, all I could think about was getting what I wanted."

Bloemetje, still floating her plant, the original Cadeau van Lavasteen, nodded and extended a hand, patting Mama's. "I know how much you wanted me. It's ok."

"We did, dear, but that's not what I'm saying this time."

"Ok." Bloemetje waited for her to continue.

"The Koningin told me what you said. About not wanting a baby."

Bloemetje's stomach tied into a knot. Must they have this conversation now? When she was in the middle of leaving her beloved?

But then Mama continued. "I want to be sure you know that it's not wrong to not want a baby. Just like it's not wrong that we wanted one so much. The only thing that's wrong is to get so caught up in what you want that you stop noticing everything that's happening around you. That you stop taking agency to do what matters. I've been thinking a lot about how you came to be with Niebie and me. I want you both to know," she glanced up at her beloved then back to their daughter, "that I agree with the fairies that Niebie taking your bloom wasn't wrong, because they didn't do it with the intent to take a child. And on Aarde they wouldn't have managed to." Niebie placed one of their hands on Mama's shoulder, and Mama placed her own over theirs, giving it a squeeze. Then they released each other. Mama continued, "But what we did do that was wrong was to agree to come colonize here."

Niebie spoke up, "It wasn't wrong of us to want a baby. Just like it's not wrong of you to not want one. But to let that want take over…it made me leave my precious budgie behind, even though I was supposed to care for him like I'd promised your Grootmoeder. But even worse, it made me agree to come settle on this land that wasn't ours to take. A great wrong that there's no justification for."

Mama nodded in agreement. "We signed on selfishly, without thinking about what it all meant. Bedrijf and all the other companies that have weaseled their way into being our culture now? They encourage people not to think. Worse, they punish people who do think things through. Because all they care about is their profit. But I shouldn't have gotten so caught up in my own wants that I stopped caring about everything going on around me."

Niebie knelt down next to Mama. "Neither of us should have. Bloemetje, we have a responsibility to do what's right…"

"…even if it takes away what we want the most in the whole universe," Mama finished Niebie's sentence, this time being the one to reach out a hand to them, placing it on their knee.

Tears welled up in Bloemetje's eyes, and she sniffled.

"I don't know how we got a daughter who already understands that at such a young age. But we did." Niebie said.

"And I needed you...both of you...to know that I've changed." Mama's voice cracked as she tried and failed to hold back a tear.

"We're so proud of you, Bloemetje. And we're sorry that you don't get to be with your first beloved forever." Niebie reached out a fingertip and brushed a tear off Bloemetje's cheek.

"Thank you." Bloemetje said. They both started to stand but she stopped them. "Wait. I need you to know that even though I'll seek out my fairy parents when we get to Aarde, you'll never stop being Mama and Niebie to me."

And now Niebie's tears joined Bloemetje's and Mama's. They stood together in the hall for a moment.

Then Bloemetje wiped her eyes on the back of her sleeve. "Ok, enough of this. It's time for us to head home." So they continued down the hall to the active flight room.

The comrades were lucky that the original flight's copilots had agreed to be on their side. Their back-up plan for flying the ship was for the most appropriate comrade to read the manual and pray. This was far superior.

The active flight room had rows of chairs with seat belts. Some of the chairs had boxes full of packing peanuts. The fairies placed the precious bulbs into these, then climbed in after them. Niebie didn't like this part of the plan, but the Koningin reassured them that this was the way she and the Oppas had arrived to begin with. It was safe enough with fairy wishes to maintain just enough gravity not to float away during take-off and until they reached cruising with the ship's gravity activated. So the humans put the lids on and buckled the boxes in. Then they settled into their own seats. As Mama's buckle clicked into place, Niebie reached out and squeezed her hand. "It's all going to be ok."

Mama gazed at them. "Even if it's not, I feel better than I have in years." She glanced at the boxes of fairies and their equally precious Cadeau van Lavasteen cargo. "I never realized before how deep down I actually felt badly about the life we were building. Now...even though I'll always feel guilt over the wrongs we've committed, I'm still able to feel good about the new life we're trying to build. If it fails, at least we tried."

Niebie nodded, a glisten remaining in their eyes even though tears were no longer falling.

Just across the aisle in one of the boxes, Bloemetje nestled into her packing peanuts, giggling with Zineke. There was no one else she would have chosen to travel to Aarde with, although she was surprised when Zineke also selected her as her companion for the trip. She expected someone as warm and kind as Zineke to have many other, closer friends. "I do have a lot of friends, you're right about that, but none of them need me for the trip as much as you do," Rineke told her, and squeezed her hand.

Now, as Rineke babbled on excitedly about trying to find her fairy fathers when they arrived back on Aarde, Bloemetje's mind wandered to another type of fairy with four red eyes, tentacles, and wings.

"What will you do?" Rineke asked, bringing her back to the present moment.

"Hm?"

"On Aarde?"

She hugged a packing peanut to her, as she saw a beautiful vision of the future that she tried to describe. "I'll teach everyone - human and fairy - about the Cadeau van Lavasteen. How unexpectedly beautiful things can happen, even out of the ashes of horrible wrongs. And how that should make us all want to do better from the start."

Then the ship rumbled as it blasted off from Lavasteen, never to return.

Afterword

If you enjoyed this book, please take a moment to give it a rating and a review. Thank you!

You may find a complete list of my work on my website:

https://opinionsofawolf.com/publications/

To stay up to date on my new publications, please consider signing up for my newsletter:

https://opinionsofawolf.com/newsletter/

A portion of proceeds from this book will be donated to the Massachusetts Center for Native American Awareness, a Native American-led 501(c)(3) nonprofit.